LEGO City ADVENTURES
CALLING ALL CARS!

By Sonia Sander
Illustrated by Mada Design

SCHOLASTIC INC.

NEW YORK   TORONTO   LONDON   AUCKLAND
SYDNEY   MEXICO CITY   NEW DELHI   HONG KONG

No part of this publication may be reproduced or stored in a retrieval system, or transmitted in any form or by any means, electronic, mechanical, photocopying, recording, or otherwise, without written permission of the publisher. For information regarding permission, write to Scholastic Inc., Attention: Permissions Department, 557 Broadway, New York, NY 10012.

ISBN 978-0-545-15523-6

LEGO, the LEGO logo, the Brick and the Knob configurations and the Minifigure are trademarks of the LEGO Group. © 2010 The LEGO Group. All rights reserved.

Published by Scholastic Inc. SCHOLASTIC and associated logos are trademarks and/or registered trademarks of Scholastic Inc.

Used under license by Scholastic Inc. All rights reserved. Published by Scholastic Inc. SCHOLASTIC and associated logos are trademarks and/or registered trademarks of Scholastic Inc.

Lexile is a registered trademark of MetaMetrics, Inc.

20 19 18   13 14 15/0

Designed by Henry Ng

Printed in U.S.A.
First printing, January 2010

The police race to the bank. Lights flash and sirens blare.